T0142416

ISAAC'S STORY

Young Carers Series

BRENDAH GAINE

© 2022 Brendah Gaine. All rights reserved.

No part of this book may be reproduced, stored in a retrieval system, or transmitted by any means without the written permission of the author.

AuthorHouse™ UK
1663 Liberty Drive
Bloomington, IN 47403 USA
www.authorhouse.co.uk
UK TFN: 0800 0148641 (Toll Free inside the UK)
UK Local: 02036 956322 (+44 20 3695 6322 from outside the UK)

Because of the dynamic nature of the Internet, any web addresses or links contained in this book may have changed since publication and may no longer be valid. The views expressed in this work are solely those of the author and do not necessarily reflect the views of the publisher, and the publisher hereby disclaims any responsibility for them.

Any people depicted in stock imagery provided by Getty Images are models, and such images are being used for illustrative purposes only.
Certain stock imagery © Getty Images.

This book is printed on acid-free paper.

ISBN: 978-1-6655-9768-5 (sc)
ISBN: 978-1-6655-9769-2 (e)

Print information available on the last page.

Published by AuthorHouse 04/13/2022

authorHOUSE

FOREWORD

These three stories written by Brendah Gaine, of children acting as carers, in a family struggling with difficulties, demonstrates the importance of a kind, compassionate and reassuring adult to whom the child can turn for help. The stories offer a creative means of helping to open up discussion, giving the child an opportunity to identify with the characters. Young carers often speak about the sense of their fear, worry and responsibility as well as isolation from peers.

Additionally, in one of the stories there is mention of the impact on school work. All this shows how important it is to give a voice to the child. In each story there is a child protection element and therefore a statutory responsibility to refer to the relevant agency so that these issues can be addressed first and foremost. In one of the stories the teacher acknowledges the courage of the child in asking for help. The boy has to overcome his fear of something calamitous happening for speaking up. The role of the adult is a skilled, delicate and patient one and the notes at the end of the stories emphasise the importance of the discussions.

Creative ideas and mindfulness exercises are suggested to help the child process and overcome the trauma of shouldering the family difficulties and these ideas are suggested with the child alongside the trusted adult. In one of the stories there is a delightful example of support and a fun outing for the whole family and this reassurance is another example of the weight of responsibility being lifted from the child's shoulders. Brendah offers an insight born out of many years of professional practice, including teaching and work with children and families through psychotherapy. The stories are grounded in authenticity and truth and would be a welcome and valuable additional resource in a variety of settings including a therapeutic one.

Helen Trevor Davies BA, CQSW (Certificate of Social Work) Goldsmiths
Retired Social Worker, Child and Adolescent Mental Health Service, Enfield
Former Child Protection Officer, NSPCC

ACKNOWLEDGEMENTS

My thanks go to the families who helped me to listen to their struggles and together we worked on solutions to learn to cope both emotionally and practically. I also want to thank Helen Trevor Davies for her carefully worded foreword. As always, I thank David and Megan for supporting me with the technological hurdles.

There once was a boy called Isaac who lived with his aunt in a small house not far from a big town. Isaac had a brother and sister and usually lived with his mom and dad. It wasn't easy for Isaac as he felt responsible for his sister and brother when his parents weren't there. He was 13 years old and was really a young carer to his younger brother and sister. Sometimes, his Dad would come home before his Mom and he would be very cross because his mom wasn't home and his Dad wanted food. Dad had been out all day and he hadn't eaten any dinner. He was hungry and expected food to be ready.

Isaac would try to find money around the house. Sometimes, he was lucky and found some loose change and he would run to the fish and chips shop and buy some chips for his Dad to eat. The children were also hungry but there was never enough money for him to buy food for everyone. It was only if Dad had fallen asleep while he was at the shop that the children had a chance to eat. Sometimes Dad was in such a bad mood that he would throw the chips back at Isaac and then the children would wait until he was out of the room and they could share what was left.

The biggest thing that worried Isaac was when mom came home from work and dad was angry and used to shout and swear a lot at her. But even worse than that was when dad would hit Mom. She would scream and ask him to stop but he had such a bad temper that her shouts made him even angrier and then he would start kicking her. It was terrible to see and Isaac felt angry and sad but worst of all he felt bad that he couldn't help his Mom. He felt responsible for his mom and brother and sister who were upset to see mom getting hurt.

He went to stay with his aunt not far away as he was so upset to see his parents fighting and arguing. But, he didn't feel good inside. He told his teacher that he felt angry and hurt at the same time especially when the children teased him. In fact, he felt angry and didn't want to hurt anyone so he threw books around the classroom and threw chairs and tables across the floor and tore up papers to get rid of the angry feelings.

But it didn't help because as he became angry he remembered the way his father hurt his mother and it made him feel very bad. His teacher told him that the memories he had were not unusual for someone who had had such bad experiences as he had. She also said that he had suffered something called trauma and could be helped to cope, with help from someone who supported children with experiences like his.

"So other children also have experiences like this?" asked Isaac.

"Yes," said his teacher. "There are other parents who treat their children badly but there is help. If you are willing to talk about it."

"If I tell you, can you help me?"

"I will certainly show you some easy things to practice so that you will feel better about yourself when these bad memories come back into your mind."

"That will be good. I will certainly try," said Isaac.

The first thing we will do is to learn to sit as still as a frog.

Isaac thought this is strange. "Why a frog?" he asked

Frogs are remarkable creatures. Frogs are able to do enormous leaps, but they can also sit very, very still. Although a frog sits still, it also knows what is going on around him, but the frog does not react straight away. The frog sits still and breathes, saving all its energy instead of using its energy up by taking notice of all the ideas that keep popping up in its head. The frog sits very still while it breathes. The frog's tummy rises and falls while it breathes.

Anything a frog can do you can do too.

All you need do is sit still and pay attention to the way your breath makes your tummy go up and down. Sit still in a quiet place and watch your breath go in and out of your body and your tummy go up and down.

Sit still like this for a few minutes and then notice how much calmer you feel. You have no time to feel anything else when you just notice your breath. You won't feel angry, you won't feel bad you will just feel calm.

Practice this every day as often as you want to and you will feel different.

Isaac was very keen to try this out at home after his teacher showed him what to do.

He told his aunt about the conversation with his teacher and he told her about sitting still like a frog and breathing.

His aunt felt it was an interesting thing to do also. They practiced together every day.

"This feels good," said Isaac. His aunt agreed.

"Let's see if we can learn other ways to help ourselves," the teacher suggested after a week of "doing the frog exercise."

The teacher was very pleased that Isaac had been practising AND had taught his aunt what to do.

"It's so good that you practised with your aunt now you both know how to feel calm," his teacher said. Now we can learn something else that will help you tell how you're feeling inside and what you can do to know how your inner feelings can be calmed down.

Your weather report.

It is about holding your finger one at a time when you uncomfortable and good feelings:

So hold your little finger and imagine a rain cloud which represent your tears. Breathe in and out slowly 3 times

Next, you can hold your ring finger and imagine small clouds and a few light raindrops when you worry about what's happening to you and your family. Do the same breathing exercise three times while you breathe in and out.

If you're feeling angry, hold your middle finger and picture a dark cloud with lightening as in a dark storm. Hold your finger and breathe in and out quite a few times until you calm down.

Now hold your pointy finger and imagine there are clear skies and sunshine and you feel warm and powerful. As you hold your finger enjoy the feeling of power. Do the breathing exercise three times and feel good.

Then hold your thumb and imagine the sun is shining brightly and you really feel happy. Do the breathing exercise three times and enjoy the strong feeling.

It's called your personal weather report.

You will be able to talk about how you're feeling inside by comparing it to

- Rainy if you feel sad and want to cry
- Overcast, cloudy and dull if you are worried
- Stormy if you feel angry

- Sunny if you feel relaxed and powerful
- Very strong with bright sunshine if you are happy

So, sit down comfortably somewhere.

Close your eyes or half close your eyes as if you are dreamy.

Notice how you are feeling inside right now.

Does it feel rainy and cloudy as if you want to cry?

Are you worried so there are grey clouds?

Is there a storm brewing inside as if you are getting angry and want to shout and kick things?

Do you feel relaxed and sunny inside as if you want to smile?

Are you happy as if the strong sun is making you feel strong?

What do you notice? How is the weather feeling inside you?

Just think what the weather is like at this moment and just let it be,.... once you know .....there is no need to do anything.....you do not need to feel any differently.....the weather is just as it is.....You cannot change the weather outside anyway, can you? So you don't need to change the weather inside. Just let it be. It will change with your breathing.

Now just think about the rain, clouds, thunderstorm or sunny skies you are noticing in your body. Be interested in what and how you are feeling. How it is right now is exactly as you are feeling. You cannot change the weather and you cannot change the mood you are feeling.

Just breathe normally and watch your belly going up on an in breath and out on an out breath. Do this for about 5 breaths then stay sitting quietly.

Later today, the weather will change and be completely different......but right now you feel the weather as it is and that's fine.

Moods change, the weather changes. You don't have to do anything....
what a relief!!!!

Now open your eyes and report what the weather is like right now.
Accept it as it is. That's fine.

"Try this exercise out with the breathing over the week and let's see how
you are at the end of next week," said the teacher.

Isaac was very pleased to go home and share with his aunt the new
things to practice.

This story is to highlight how a child has to take responsibility for younger siblings when parents are irresponsible. It also emphasises the need to ask for help when the feelings that a young carer feels gets out of hand.

It shows that you can learn to help yourself and control your feelings by learning techniques like Isaac did.

Questions for adults to discuss with children

Did the story teach you anything about Isaac's family?

How did you feel when you read about the treatment of his dad towards his mum?

What would you have done?

Why don't you try these ways to help you feel differently and practice like Isaac if you feel angry and want to feel differently?

Printed in the United States
by Baker & Taylor Publisher Services